I0684173

SURFSIDE
Tales of the fantastic Maine coast

Sharon Lee

Pinbeam Books
http://www.pinbeambooks.com

This is a work of fiction. All the characters and events portrayed in this novel are fiction or are used fictitiously.

COPYRIGHT PAGE

Surfside

Copyright © 2012, 2013 by **Sharon Lee**. All rights reserved. No part of this publication may be reproduced or transmitted in any form or by any means, electronic or mechanical, without permission in writing from the author. Please remember that distributing an author's work without permission or payment is theft; and that the authors whose works sell best are those most likely to let us publish more of their works.

Emancipated Child first published at Splinter Universe (www.splinteruniverse.com), July 2012

How Nathan Archer Came to be a Prince of the Land of the Flowers first published at Splinter Universe (www.splinteruniverse.com), September 2012

In Which Writing Novels is Like Sewing, is original to this publication

ISBN: 978-1-948465-00-7

Published August 2013 by Pinbeam Books

Pinbeam Books

PO Box 1586

Waterville ME 04903

email info@pinbeambooks.com

Cover image from JupiterImages

Cover design by Sharon Lee

FOREWORD

In Which Writing Novels is Like Sewing
OR
Where Short Stories Come From

Now, what I'm about to tell you is true—but, like so many things about and of writing, it's not the only truth. And it's certainly not a universal truth. It's a truth that's true for me, as a writer.

Sometimes.

Here it is in a nutshell—I often find that, when I come to the "end" of a novel or series of novels, I'm likely to have bits and pieces of story or character "left over," sort of like the sequins and scraps of fabric left over from a sewing project.

For instance, I'll have in my head the story of a secondary character from the novel; a story that may *connect*, or even intersect, with the novel, but which by no means is essential to the story told, or the problem solved, within the novel. It may be a story that has no relation to the novel at all; stories that could have—no, check that. Stories that *did happen*, only slightly to the left of the stage, in the corners and quiet places cast in the shadows of the novel's reality.

Sometimes those stories *absolutely must be written*; I have no say in the matter. If I come up stubborn, pleading press of other (paying) work, then the story will just sit there, clogging up my brain, until I knuckle under and write it down. Sometimes—most often, I'd say—the leftovers, the could-be stories fade, and melt down into the bedrock, where they add an extra layer of verisimilitude to the novel's worldbuilding.

What you have here, in *Surfside*, is a mixed bag of sparkly scraps; two stories that spun out of *Carousel Tides,* the first book in the Archers Beach trilogy, published by Baen Books.

3

Carousel Tides is a contemporary fantasy set in the fictional town of Archers Beach, Maine. That novel involved quite a bit of world-building, especially regarding the hierarchy of magics available to the characters, and the rules by which each sort of magic operates. The most basic sort of magic is available to the *trenvay,* who are each responsible for a bit of land, or marsh, a tree, or a rock. The next level up is the land magic available to the Guardian of the land, a sort of uber-*trenvay.* All three Carousel books (*Carousel Tides, Carousel Sun, Carousel Seas*) are told in first-person by Kate Archer, the Guardian of Archers Beach.

In the course of working on Kate's story—the story of a Guardian who deserted her duty, and returned to it years later—it occurred to me to wonder how other Guardians might arise, and how they would view and dispatch their duties. How, in essence, someone would come to accept a bond and a responsibility that is *magical,* in this day of Android phones and cloud computing.

The first story in this chapbook, "Emacipated Child," offers. . .one. . .answer to that set of questions. It's set in the very tiny town of Surfside, right next to Archers Beach. Kate Archer makes a brief appearance, but this is Jason's story to tell.

The second story is in fact an outtake from *Carousel Tides*; a little bit of Kate Archer's family history.

#

Let me tell you just a little bit about Archers Beach, Maine, if I may.

Archers Beach is a town that's almost real. Magic works in Archers Beach—to an extent—and it is the site of the World Gate, which connects our own World with five other Worlds.

The history, coastline, and geography of Archers Beach were constructed—cut, and paired, and pieced—out of the whole cloth of the Maine coastal towns of Old Orchard Beach, Ocean Park, Kinney Shores, Camp Ellis, and also the Rachel Carson National Wildlife Refuge.

For more information about Archers Beach, please visit the Carousel Tides website (www.carouseltides.com), or The Archers Beach Photo-Diary on Pinterest (pinterest.com/rolanni/archers-beach-diary/)

The Archers Beach Trilogy consists of three novels:

Carousel Tides, Baen Books, November 2010

Carousel Sun, Baen Books, February 2014

Carousel Seas, Baen Books, January 2015

—Sharon Lee
Cat Farm and Confusion Factory
amended July 2016

Emancipated Child

An Archers Beach Story
by
Sharon Lee

Jason's lungs were on fire, and he could hear Matt's sneakers pounding on the trail behind him over the harsh rasp of his breath. Matt was taller than he was, and on the track team, but Jason had a head start.

"Too good for us, you little bastard? I'll show you too good!"

It was worrisome that Matt had breath left over from running to yell with. Jason couldn't have answered if he wanted to, which he didn't. All he wanted to do was to get the hell gone, out of Matt's range – which wasn't going to happen, so the next best thing was to get to the store, where there would be people – or at least Johnna. Not even Matt was stupid enough to beat up somebody in front of a witness.

On the right he saw the short-cut that took a corner off the main trail and would put him in the store's parking lot in a couple of minutes.

Assuming Matt didn't catch him first.

Jason took the turn into the shortcut hard, sand and pebbles skidding underfoot. He took a hard breath and felt it come easier, deeper, even as his short legs found a renewed burst of speed.

Second wind, he thought, pelting down the thin trail between high walls of cat-tail and swamp grass. He could still hear Matt behind him, but it sounded like his cousin hadn't found his own second wind.

In fact, it sounded like he was laboring, his pursuing footsteps not pounding so much as. . .sliding; almost as if the sand were loose, rather than packed down hard.

Jason ran on, fists pumping, breathing hard, but not gasping, suddenly feeling as if he could keep on running forever. He took a curve in the path at speed, dodging the skinny dead tree that made the way even thinner.

Must be that runner's high the jocks talked about.

Jason flew on.

"Hey!" Matt yelled from behind him, surprise sounding amidst a loud crack and a clatter like sticks being flung onto stone. "Hey, ow!"

Ow?

Jason slowed, and dared to look back over his shoulder. Matt might be going to kill him, but they were cousins, and if he was *really* hurt –

He got one glimpse of the old tree, now missing the limb that had overhung the path, and Matt pushing himself to his knees. If that limb had hit –

This way!

His sleeve was snatched and he was yanked to the right, through a tangle of dry reeds and out again into a small grassy place, hemmed in with ash and marsh willow.

Jason staggered to a stop, feeling damp and exhausted. Before him, a grey stone thrust out of the grass. Jason collapsed onto its conveniently flat top as if it were a stool, closed his eyes and waited for his heart-rate to come down. He strained his ears, but he didn't hear any signs of pursuit, which made him wonder again if his cousin was hurt.

And how much he cared.

"I've got to get to work pretty soon," he said outloud to the glade in general.

There was no response, unless you counted the sudden whistle of a red-wing blackbird. He hadn't really expected a response, but he did try to be polite. His dad, back before the cancer, had said that it was the least a man who heard voices could do, was to be polite.

The voices themselves – well. He'd heard them his whole life, sometimes direct, like the one that had yelled at him to get off the trail *this way*. Mostly, though, they were a comfortable background noise. The voices were company, sort of, like a radio playing somewhere in the house made you feel less alone.

"Why does he hate you?" a rough voice asked then – an outloud voice, not at all like the voices in his head, and one Jason had never heard before.

He turned his head, carefully.

A girl was leaning against a swamp maple, arms crossed over her chest. She might've been his age, her face was brown, and her hair, too. She was wearing a bottle green t-shirt and brown cargo pants. Her eyes were the same green as her t-shirt.

Not somebody he knew, and he knew everybody in Surfside. 'Course, there wasn't any law said she couldn't've come across the walking path higher up in the main marsh; or down, from Scarborough; or up, from Archers Beach.

"Well," Jason said carefully. "He doesn't really *hate* me so much as he's pretty mad at me."

The girl's eyebrows lifted.

"Why is he pretty mad, then?"

None of your business, was on the tip of his tongue, but. . .he had a. . .*feeling*.

Besides, it wasn't like it was a state secret.

"He's mad 'cause I'm emancipated," he said. "His folks and him figure that means I think I'm too good for them."

"What is emancipated?" she asked, which he could've predicted for the next question. *Everybody* asked that one.

"It means I petitioned the court to be able to – to leave my parent's authority and house, and to live on my own." The full legal name was *emancipated child*, which he didn't bother to say, because he was, ferchristsake, *not* a child. He was sixteen, and fully in control of his own life.

He took a breath and answered the next most common question before she could ask it.

"And the reason I did it is because my dad died and my mom. . .She moved out of town, up to Portland, and in with –"

. . .*with her coke-head boyfriend*. He swallowed that. There was such a thing as too personal, after all.

". . .with a friend. We don't get along – me and the friend—and besides I didn't want to live in Portland." He'd been sick in Portland; all the time – not bad sick, like cancer, or anything like that. Just that his head hurt, and his stomach was queasy, kinda, and he hadn't been able to hear the voices in his head over all the rush and racket.

He took another breath. "So I got a job doing handywork at the Sunspray, and I showed I was able to be independent and all."

"And that boy is angry because you are emancipated and he is not?"

Jason laughed. "No—oh, *hell* no! Matt's hot – well, I'm guessing he caught it from his mom – she's my mom's sister. They just all figured I should move in with them, see? Except that wasn't going to work, either." Because him and Matt weren't exactly best friends even when he wasn't channeling Aunt Dottie's anger – and her taste in boyfriends wasn't any better than *his* mom's, and besides that – they lived in Scarborough.

No reason to say any of that, either, to some strange girl chance-met in the marsh, so he shifted on the rock and said instead.

"I'm going to hafta get to work pretty soon."

"So that you remain emancipated." She nodded and pushed away from the tree she'd been leaning against. "I'll walk with you," she said, "to Johnna's store."

"Sure," he said, sliding off the rock.

She was taller than he was, which almost everybody was, so no surprises there; and skinny in a way that said she might've just had a growth spurt.

"I'm Jason Thibodeau," he said, as she stepped in front of him and disappeared into the wall of reeds. "By the way."

He followed her, holding an arm in front of his eyes, but it – it almost seemed like the reeds bent out of his way. There must, he told himself, be a trail – maybe a deer track – that the girl knew about and that he just didn't see.

She was waiting for him on the path, looking back the way he had come. He snuck a look that way, himself. The dead tree stood where it always had, one of its limbs down and shattered across the path.

There wasn't any sign of Matt.

Jason breathed a sigh of relief.

"Your cousin was not hurt," the girl said. "Only frightened."

"That's good," he said, and added, "though I can't think of much that would scare Matt."

She snorted lightly, maybe it was a laugh, and turned toward Johnna's store, walking to the left of the path and slightly ahead of him.

"What's your name?" Jason asked, after they'd gone a couple dozen steps in silence.

She glanced at him over her shoulder – a flash of green eyes behind rough brown hair.

"Cedar," she said. "Cedar White."

"You live around here?"

She snorted another laugh. "Oh, yes."

"New?" he asked, which people from Away might think was rude, he remembered, and added a reason for why he might care. "Hadn't seen you in school, is all."

"Ah," she said, and gave him another, slower, look from behind her hair. "I am home schooled."

That set a tingle up his nerves – a lie if he'd ever heard one. He could tell, usually, when people were telling the truth. Still, lying about being home-schooled didn't prove she was a runaway – that? Was probably his own nerves talking, since he'd put some thought into what he'd do, and where he'd go, while he was waiting for the court to decide his case, knowing how slim his chances were for a win, and if he had the guts to run away, if he didn't win.

Lucky for him, it hadn't come to that, because where would he have run to, except back to Surfside, year-round population just six souls under 200, and no place at all to hide?

The path widened into a dirt parking lot. Jason stretched his legs so he was walking beside Cedar and then had to drop back again as she went mounted the step onto the porch, opened the door, stepped inside – and paused, the door balanced on brown fingertips.

He grabbed it hurriedly. "Thanks."

Johnna was working in the front of the middle cooler – making sure the beer was stocked and cold for the home-coming crew, Jason knew. She looked 'round when the bell rang and straightened.

"You want something?" she asked, glaring at Cedar.

The girl nodded. "Work."

"An' you figure *I* got work?" Johnna shook her head and looked over Cedar's shoulder to Jason.

"Cousin of yours in here, says to let you know, if you should happen by, that he'll see you in school tomorrow."

"Thanks." He slipped past Cedar, opened up the front cooler, pulled out a can of root beer and a premade ham sandwich on white bread.

"That all you havin' for supper, boy?" Johnna asked him, like she did every day.

He shook his head, like he did every day. "Just to get me through work," he said. "I'll have supper when I get home."

"You see you do. Vegetables, I'm talking."

"Carrots," he promised her, fishing a couple dollar bills out of his jeans pocket. He put them on the counter by the register, then looked to the girl, standing silent to one side.

"You need something to eat?" he asked her. "It's on me."

She blinked green eyes at him, the side of her mouth turning up like she'd tasted something bad.

"You never mind 'bout her," Johnna said, letting the door to the cooler thump shut. "Dinner comes with the shift." She gave Cedar another glare, not exactly, Jason thought, friendly, before she turned it on him.

"You'd best get on 'fore Vonny dings you for being late."

Jason sighed and gathered up his soda and sandwich. While he'd been lucky to get the job at the Sunspray, there wasn't any sense in pretending that Bob Varney, his boss, was anything but a mean sonofabitch. He'd greeted the news of Jason's successful emancipation with a frown and a look in his eye that Jason just knew meant he was thinking about how much grief and trouble he could cause, if he turned the kid off, since staying employed was one of the major terms of his independence. If Jason lost his job, he was supposed to report himself to the Department of Health and Human Services, so he could be placed in a foster home.

Like he was *that* dumb.

"I'm going," he told Johnna, and gave Cedar a nod.

"Thanks," he said to her.

It wasn't until he was across the road and sprinting down the Sunspray's long drive that he wondered what he'd been thanking her for.

#

It had been yard work today – Jason's favorite and the primary reason Mr. Varney'd taken him on. Mr. Varney was an electrician by trade, with some carpentry and plumbing on the side – a true handyman. What he had no feeling or care for, was plants and lawns and trees, so all that sort of thing fell to Jason. Since it also kept him out of his boss' way – and under his radar – it was all good as far as Jason was concerned.

Work of the day had been putting down pine chips around the tree trunks, and in the two big gardens at the front of the building.

He put his back into it, enjoying the breeze, the early-spring lack of bugs, the scent of the wood chips, and the easy, familiar murmur of the voices in his head.

When his watch beeped the half-shift warning, he left his tools and the wheelbarrow where they were, grabbed his sandwich and root beer and walked to the back of the building, letting himself out by the beach-gate.

What had been a breeze inside the protected grounds was a wind here on the sand, running toward the shore on the back of the incoming tide. Jason crossed the dunes on the board walkway, and turned right, walking down the beach to the Rock.

The Rock was something of a landmark, and it marked the boundary between Surfside and Archers Beach, the town next door. The Rock had been one of his father's favorite places – maybe his favorite place, in town. Even when he'd barely been able to walk, he'd manage to get to the Rock, and sit down on the sand with his back against it. It made him feel better, he said, to visit with an old friend.

After his dad died, Jason hadn't visited the Rock much – he'd told himself because there'd been too much other stuff going on, but the truth – the *real* truth was that he hadn't forgiven the Rock –

Hadn't forgiven it for not saving his father.

Which was just stupid, little-kid thinking. Like a rock – no matter how old – could keep a man from dying of stomach cancer. . .

He'd made a point of visiting since he'd come back to town, most days eating his half-shift snack with his back companionably braced against the Rock's sea-washed surface. He was pretty sure the Rock understood, and forgave him for being an idiot.

Today, he leaned against the leeward side of the Rock while he ate his sandwich. He balled up the wrapping and stuck it in his pocket, drained his root beer, stuck the empty in his other pocket, and headed back to the Sunspray, feeling peaceable and content.

It wasn't far – nothing in Surfside was very far from anything else; it was only a little strip of land between Archers Beach and Pine Point – a silly little bit of land that nobody wanted, nestled between the marsh and the sea. The Sunspray was the biggest – and newest – thing in Surfside, hardly ten years old. Before the Sunspray, there'd been an old "tourist resort" on the land, built 'way back at the end of World War I. People from Away would take a train up to Archers Beach, then, that's what Johnna'd told him, and some of them would ride the trolley out to the tourist resort.

Now, people from Away drove up in their Infinitis, their BMWs, and their Lexuses, to their condo summer homes, swelling Surfside's population to almost three hundred for the ten or twelve weeks of summer.

There wasn't much to do in Surfside, of course, outside of laying on the beach. The excitement was down in Archers Beach, with its amusement park, and the Pier; the bars and restaurants. If you wanted a beer in Surfside, you bought a six-pack at Johnna's store; if you wanted to eat in a restaurant, you went someplace else.

He was walking briskly; the Sunspray's boardwalk, with its all-weather grey paint and railings on both sides, was just ahead. On his right was the utility shed where the Sunspray kept beach chairs and umbrellas for its residents, the door swinging in wind off the sea.

Jason frowned. The door was supposed to be padlocked, and Mr. Varney held the key. He guessed one of the hinges could have rusted through, but –

But, no, he saw, as he reached the shed. The padlock was through one metal hasp, but not through both. If Mr. Varney'd been in a hurry, that might explain it, though why he'd be in the shed at this time of year. . .

Jason grabbed the door, automatically pulling it wide, to make sure that the chairs were in place.

They were.

And piled around and on top of them were a number of what looked to be bricks, wrapped in black plastic – and they didn't belong there, at all.

#

"OK, back to work," Mr. Varney said, snapping the lock through both hasps and yanking on it hard to make sure it had caught.

"But," Jason said, "what are those things?"

His boss gave him a hard stare.

"Stuff I'm holding for a friend, all right? Be gone in a day er two. Nothin' to do with you, and nothin' to be blabbing about to Sodeby, neither."

Mr. Sodeby was the site manager. Mr. Varney's boss.

There was probably a policy against Mr. Varney using Sunspray property to store "things" for a friend. On the other hand, Mr. Varney could fire him, and *then* where would he be?

So – "Sure," he said.

#

Nobody was chasing him today—nobody had to. Matt had gotten in some good licks right after gym, with the help of Danny Walker, who'd tripped him, and then, when he was getting up, after Matt was done with him, had casually slammed him into the wall.

He'd staggered in after them, heading for the nearest bathroom, and hadn't quite gotten all the blood off his face when the door opened and Mr. Marks, the principal, walked in.

So, on top of a black eye, a wrenched knee, and a very sore stomach, he had Saturday detention.

For fighting on school property.

He stepped from the main trail onto the Surfside trail, limping, and shook his head. Things might've gone a little easier with Mr. Marks, if he'd said who he'd been fighting *with*, which he hadn't done, not even when the threat of suspension had been brought out.

First of all—it was a bogus threat; Mr. Marks would look a right fool for suspending a kid for fighting with himself. Especially an honor-roll kid.

Second—wouldn't Matt just kill him *dead* if he squealed.

So, now he was going to have to negotiate with Mr. Varney for four morning hours off on Saturday, his only full-work-day, and right when there was the spring yard work to do. It was staying light now until seven, seven-thirty, so he figured he could pick up a couple of the Saturday hours in the evening—and maybe work late on Friday, too. That was what he'd offer Varney.

He rounded the bend in the path with a heartfelt sigh. Almost there; the shortcut was just up ahead—

And there was somebody waiting on the edge of the path.

Jason tensed, not recognizing the shadow against the weeds, and knowing for sure he wasn't running any—

The figure turned, stepped full into the path and came toward him.

Jason let his breath out in a rush.

"Cedar White, hey," he said, as nonchalantly as he could.

She stopped in the middle of the trail, her hands on her hips, and a frown on her face.

"What happened to you?"

"Well." Since she was blocking the trail, he stopped, too. "My cousin saw me in school today, like he told Johnna to tell me he would."

"And he tried to kill you."

He shook his head. "Just make me sorry." He sighed. "Which I am. Sorry on all fronts, looks like. Got Saturday detention for fighting on school grounds, so I need to convince Mr. Varney to let me work late on Friday and late on Saturday, to make up the time." He closed his eyes. Opened them. "Which means I've gotta move on, if you don't mind."

She didn't take the hint. "If you accepted your power, these things would not happen to you," she said.

He blinked at her. "Accept my *power*?" He opened his arms wide. "Do I look like somebody who has *power* to you?"

"In fact," she said, suddenly moving to one side of the trail, "you do. You look to me like the Guardian of this land. Don't you hear it talking to you? Don't you hear *me* talking to you?"

He had started walking again—almost stopped, and satisfied himself with sending her a hard stare.

"I hear *you* talking to me because *you're talking to me*," he said, and didn't ask, *How do you know about the voices? Do you hear them, too?*

She walked beside him, keeping pace with his limp.

"I could help you more if you accepted the land," she said, as they crossed the parking lot. "Johnna could, and others of the *trenvay*."

Great. Yesterday, he'd met a girl. She was weird, but who wasn't? Today, she let him know that she was a total nutcase.

No, he thought, painfully, that's not fair. After all, his father hadn't laughed at him when he said he heard voices. His father, who had counted a big old beach rock as one of his longest and best friends.

He sighed.

"Do you hear the voices?" he asked her.

Her mouth bent a little. He thought it might've been her version of a smile.

"I'm not the Guardian," she said; "I'm *trenvay*."

She went up the stairs ahead of him, opened the door, stepped through and stood holding it open for him.

"Thanks," he said. And, "What's that, exactly? *Trenvay?*"

"In my case, it means I live in a tree," she said. "Other *trenvay* have other...

arrangements." Another sharp green stare from behind her hair. "Didn't your father tell you these things?"

"His father," Johnna said, from behind the counter, "din't more'n half believe, himself. Not so much gave himself to the land, as accepted he was a little touched in the head." She nodded at Jason. "It was a bad day when you told him you heard voices. Figured you'd inherited, which you had. Sat here on the floor with his back against the counter, just drinking beer right outta my cooler and crying like a little baby."

"My dad thought I was nuts?" Jason asked. "Just like him?"

"That's it. Should've known better, but his grandma—goin' back now a good number of years, to the buildin' of the old resort—his grandma died early, leaving a baby an' a husband who was deafer'n a barn door. The baby—his ma—she talked about what she heard, but she din't have the lore. Her pa finally took her off to Portland for a cure. She come back. . .broke. Married who he said, then did what <u>he</u> said. Had a baby—your dad—then. . .just faded into the wind. I seen <u>trenvay</u> go that way, a time or two, but never a mortal creature. Your dad, all he knew was that his ma'd heard things and gotten trouble for it, so he din't ever say, nor ask no questions." She sighed and shook her head.

"We been without a long time, Jason. It'd be good—for the land, and the *trenvay*—"

"And him," Cedar said, moving to the cooler and pulling out a wrapped ham sandwich and a root beer. She put them on the counter and looked hard at Johnna. "*And him.* Don't forget that."

"Some things'll be easier," said Johnna, looking stubborn. "Other things, won't."

"Sounds like life," Jason said, shaking his head. "Look, unless being—what? Guardian?—is something I can put on my resume and show the DHS if they ask am I employed, I'm going to have to pass, and—" he glanced to the clock on the back wall—"get to work."

He reached into his pocket, and stopped when Johnna waved a hand. "Get on with ya."

"I'll carry," Cedar said, snatching up the root beer and sandwich. "You walk."

They were half-way up the Sunspray's drive when he asked her, feeling like an idiot.

"So, how would I go about accepting my power, assuming I have any?"

She shook her hair back out of her face and gave him a straight look. Her eyes, he saw—the brilliant, bright green wasn't the oddest thing about them. The oddest thing about them was that they didn't have any whites—they were green, with dark rings.

Not. . .regular. . .human. . .eyes.

"To accept your power, you only need to reach to the land, and welcome it in," she said.

Right.

"Sounds simple enough. I'll try it one day when I'm bored," he said, mildly.

They were at the maintenance entrance. He turned, painfully, and held out his hands.

"Thanks for carrying. I'll take it from here."

She handed over the sandwich and root beer without a word, and turned away. He used his key in the lock, and pushed the door open, wincing at the protest of bruises.

When he looked down the drive, Cedar was nowhere to be seen.

#

Mr. Varney wasn't in the office, or in any of his other usual places. Jason sighed, half in relief and half in frustration, clocked in, grabbed his shovel and rake, and went out to the back where the pile of pine bark and the wheelbarrow waited for him.

By the time he'd gotten the chips in the barrow, and the barrow around the side, he was sweating and shivering. Stupid.

He had to do his job. *Had* to. Bad enough to have to talk to Varney about shifting his work hours around the detention. But if it looked like he was slacking off. . .

"Sit down," said a rough, familiar voice, "and tell me what to do."

He looked up into Cedar's unhuman green eyes.

"I've got to put the chips around the base of the trees, to keep the weeds down."

"I will do it," she said, taking the shovel out of his hand. "You will sit down on that wall and supervise me."

"I don't—"

"I know," she interrupted, turning to the wheelbarrow, "a very great deal about trees."

#

She was a willing worker, and strong, too. He had to get up twice, to show her how to rake the chips into neat, unnatural circles, so that nothing untidy upset the eyes of the Sunspray's residents. She pursed her lips, and he got a feeling like she wasn't exactly pleased with the idea, but she *got it*, and raked.

He watched her, and. . .dozed.

Immediately he closed his eyes, the constant background hum of the voices increased, and he felt a. . .drawing-in, as if friends were coming close around him, to shield him from the wind. He sighed, comforted and. . .safe.

Safe.

Now, wasn't that a peculiar feeling.

"Jason."

He opened his eyes, looking directly into Cedar's face.

"What?" he asked, groggily, then panic took him, chasing away the residual feeling of *safe*. "Is Mr. Varney back?"

"I don't know," she answered carelessly. "What I do know is *that* tree is sick." She raised an arm and pointed.

He squinted along the line of her arm to a grey birch.

"It looks all right to me."

"It might look all right," she said sharply. "But it's not. You can cure it."

He blinked at her.

"No, I can't."

"Yes," she said, the *ess* a positive hiss, "you can. What's more, if you accepted your power, you could cure yourself, too."

He sighed. "Cedar, look. . ."

"Halloo!" came a shout. "Hey, Vonny! Anybody here?" This was followed by the sound of a door being pounded vigorously.

Jason came to his feet, gasping as every single one of his bruises protested, and headed.

"They better knock it off before Mr. Sodeby hears it," he said, hobbling as fast as he could toward the back of the building.

He heard an exasperated sigh, glanced to his side, and wasn't really surprised to see Cedar keeping pace with him.

"What is this to you?"

"If whoever that is doesn't quiet down, he'll draw Mr. Sodeby. Mr. Sodeby will take a chunk out of Mr. Varney, who will then take a chunk out of me. Think trickle-down economics."

They'd reached the side door by this time, just as the man started a renewed assault on the door.

"Can I help you?" Jason called, hobbling as fast as he could.

The man turned around—nobody he knew; maybe a lobsterman down from Pine Point, or a clam-digger. He was unshaven without being bearded, his sweater was rough, and his jeans were tough. He was wearing boots, scarred and salt-stained.

"I'm looking for Vonny," he said. "S'pose to meet me."

"I'm Jason Thibodeau," he said; "Mr. Varney's assistant. He's not here right now. Is there something I can help you with?"

"Well, yeah, maybe so." The man jerked his head beachward. "Need the key to that shed o'his."

Jason's heart sank. The key to the shed was on Mr. Varney's personal ring that he always had on him.

"I'm sorry," he said to the man, "I don't have access to the key. If you'd like to wait in the garden, I'll go—"

But the man had already turned away.

"Second time that sumbitch ain't here when I come by. Starting to get the feelin' he don't wanna see me. That's all right; I'll take care of it my own self."

He turned away and strode toward the dune-gate.

Jason stared after him. The beach wasn't private, exactly, but the shed—if this guy was going to vandalize the shed—

"Hey!" he yelled, limping after the man.

"Jason, he didn't want your help," Cedar said from beside him.

"Well, but—"

"And—" She pointed across the pool court, to a quick moving shadow. "Is that Mr. Varney?"

It was, Jason saw with relief, and he was moving fast for a big man. He'd left his toolbelt off, but he had a hammer in his hand. The dune-gate slammed behind the loud man. Mr. Varney waited, like he was counting, then eased the gate open just far enough so he could slip through, and kept a hand on it, so it shut again, silently.

Jason bit his lip and kept on, limping across the court with Cedar beside him.

"Why?" she demanded. "It's between them, whatever it is, and has nothing to do with you!"

He shook his head.

"Could be—I don't know, trouble. That guy was pretty mad. Don't want him to get into a fight with Mr. Varney."

"Why not?" asked Cedar, which was a good question, actually. So good that Jason decided to ignore her and shambled into a run. By the time he reached the dune-gate, the boardwalk was empty.

He opened the gate, carefully. Cedar, behind him, sighed loudly, but made sure the gate didn't smack home, and followed him down the walk, and over the dunes.

#

There was a pick-up truck parked on the far side of the umbrella shed, its nose pointed south, toward Archers Beach.

By the shed itself was the loud man, bent over the lock, working at it with—a screwdriver, maybe.

Almost immediately behind him was Mr. Varney, choking the hammer tight and raising it as he stepped forward—

Jason yelled.

The man at the shed dropped the lock and spun, lunging with—

Not a screwdriver, Jason saw—a knife.

He jumped from the end of the boardwalk into the dry sand, and flailed, his wrenched knee buckling. All at once, he found his feet, and ran toward the two men.

Mr. Varney, swung down with the hammer, striking the loud man's shoulder. He grunted, but didn't draw back. Mr. Varney swung the hammer again, and this time he connected.

The loud man fell like a tree.

Jason stopped where he was, staring at the scene before him, Mr. Varney holding the hammer, looking down at his fallen opponent, a red stain beginning to show on the side of his work shirt.

The other man. . .

Jason looked down. He wasn't bleeding, not that could be seen, but that had been a hell of a whack Mr. Varney'd—

It came to him, with the force of an irrefutable fact, that the loud man was dead.

"You killed him," he said, his voice flat.

Mr. Varney turned slowly, letting the hammer fall from his hand.

"Him?" he said, walking toward Jason. "Take more'n a tap on the head to kill him. This is gonna work out just fine."

He raised his arm. Jason staggered back, trying to twist out of the path of the descending fist—

\#

"That worked well," a familiar voice breathed in his ear. "Jason?"

He pried his eyes open against the pounding of his head.

"Cedar. Where's—"

"Another man came across the dunes in a buggy," she said, talking fast. "He's helping Mr. Varney unload packages from the shed. Mr. Varney said he would call the cops when the other man was gone, and turn you in for killing Remmy Jule. He said," she swallowed hard, and Jason, looking at her closely, saw that she was crying. "He said that would keep you out of Surfside." Her face twisted. "Damn you, Jason, why did you have to fall on the beach? The land can't help you here!"

He stared at her. Keep him out of Surfside? In jail, that would be. For murder. He'd *never* come back home, never hear the voices again.

. .

"I accept my power," he whispered, hoarsely.

Cedar shook her head violently. "Idiot! The beach is neutral! You need to *be on* the land!"

He didn't think he could move, and anyway—

"Can they see me? Varney and his friend?"

She nodded.

"What're they doing about you?"

"They don't see me—just you."

He lay there for what seemed like a really long time, hearing the men's voices, and the thump the plastic-wrapped bricks made when they landed in the back of the buggy.

"They can't see you? Because you live in a tree?"

"Because I'm calling on my tree, yes."

"Your tree," pursued Jason, and *never mind* that girls didn't live in trees, "that has roots in. . .the land?"

She stared at him, green eyes wide.

"*Yes*," she said.

"Give me your hand."

He raised his, she grabbed it in strong brown fingers.

Immediately his head was flooded with concerned voices, a sense of urgency, a need, a need—

"Hey, what the *hell*!" shouted a man's voice. "Where'd that girl come from?"

Cedar rose, and he did, brought to his feet by her implacable grip. Mr. Varney had just stepped out of the shed, bricks in hand. The other man reached into the buggy's well, and pulled out a gun.

"I accept!" Jason yelled, hanging on to Cedar's hand like it was a lifeline, feeling his roots thrust deep into the soil, and the late sun kissing his leaves. "I accept!"

And he...

He threw open his heart.

Joy filled him, the voices swelling into music inside his head. He was stone, he was tree; he was dune rose, cattail, and swamp grass. He was Jason Thibodeau.

He was Surfside.

The man by the buggy raised his gun.

Jason.. .*reached*, down below the sand into rock that was Surfside, and snapped it good and sharp, like shaking out a rag rug.

The beach heaved.

Mr. Varney was thrown right off his feet, bricks flying out of his hands. There was a thud, like maybe he'd hit his head on the shed door.

The man with the gun was thrown backward and up, the gun discharging into the air. The buggy flipped over onto its side; the man smacked into it, hard, slid down to the sand, the gun tumbling out of his slack grip, and lay still.

Jason took a deep breath, and looked into Cedar's face.

"OK?" he asked.

She nodded, green eyes glowing.

"Good. Go down to Johnna's and call the sheriff. I'll stay here in case—in case I'm needed."

"Yes," she said, and was gone, running for the boardwalk.

Jason sat down in the sand to wait, the voices singing jubilations inside his head.

#

"Well, I won't say that was the noisiest thing I ever heard in my life, but it was close."

Jason looked up sharply, seeing the three still forms on the beach, the open door of the shed moving in the sea breeze, the buggy on its side in the sand, the pick-up empty and undisturbed, some distance beyond.

And, suddenly, like a picture slowly coming into focus, a black-haired woman in jeans and a bright blue sweatshirt with the sleeves pushed to the elbow was walking toward him, along the skirt of the dune.

Jason came to his feet.

The woman stopped where she was, maybe a dozen steps out, tucked her hands into the pockets of her jeans and looked at him, head tipped to one side. *Ride the Carousel at Archers Beach*, was emblazoned across the front of her sweatshirt.

"Pretty damn' impressive," she said. "But still—noisy. What's your name?"

"Jason Thibodeau."

She nodded like she'd sort of expected that, and said, "Well, Jason Thibodeau, I'm Kate Archer, the Guardian next door."

Not too many hours ago, he would've pegged her as a crazy lady with that. Now, he only returned her nod.

"'evening," he said politely. "Sorry about the noise. I'm—new at this."

"No worries, there's only a couple who heard it. Anyhow, I'm not here to complain, but offer an assist, if you happen to need one." She turned at the waist, looking down at the carnage on the beach.

"You got this under control?"

"I think so. A. . .friend went to call the sheriff."

"Good plan. What's the story?"

Jason took a breath.

"The—the dead man, he came looking for Mr. Varney toward the mid-point of my work shift and the two of 'em went to get something out of the shed. When they didn't come back after a time, I got worried and came out to check was everything OK."

She nodded thoughtfully. "And found the scene as it lies before us. Not too bad." She stared down the beach, eyes narrowed.

"'less I miss my guess, the dead guy's Remmy Jule, one of our coastline entrepreneurs. The Jules go 'way back, smuggling. Supposing those bricks are marijuana, I don't think the sheriff's going to have any trouble figuring out what went down here."

She turned back to him, her eyes narrowing as if she'd heard something.

Another heartbeat and Jason heard it, too.

A siren.

"You want me to stay?"

He thought about that.

"Be hard to explain?"

"It would, at that," she agreed. "You'll do fine. When you get this behind you, look me up, down at the carousel. We can share Guardian tips."

He looked at her, the siren coming closer. Her eyes were green, but human green, and he blurted.

"My friend—she. . .lives in a tree."

Kate Archer nodded easily. "So's my grandmother. She tells me it's nice." She gave him a grin. "I'll leave you to business now, Guardian. Don't be a stranger, hey?"

She walked away then, keeping to the dune's edge until a wisp of sea mist swirled up and hid her from sight.

The siren shrieked into the Sunspray's parking lot, accompanied by squealing tires. He heard a car door slam, and very quickly, the sound of rapid footsteps on the boardwalk.

Jason, Surfside singing in his blood, turned to greet the sheriff.

How Nathan Archer Came to be a Prince of the Land of the Flowers

As told by Kate Archer

to Sharon Lee

You might be wondering how it was that Nathan Archer came to be one of the Sasanoa. The short answer is, he was born in the Land of the Flowers, and raised up in the house of Aeronymous, a Sea Ozali of some considerable standing.

That's the short answer. The longer answer — well, that's a tale.

Now, what you have to understand first off is that the Archers have been on this land a long, long time. Not as long as the Pepperidges, but — long enough. Some would say, too long.

There's various stories in the family about how the Archers came to be caretakers of the land. Chief Glooskap lost it in a game of dice to the first of the name to settle here — that's one. Another says, no, it was given in return for a favor — and a third still says the other two are hogwash, and what John Archer had done was to marry Glooskap's daughter, with the land being her wedding portion.

Any of those might be probable, though the giving and losing of land would've been an idea more comfortable with Irish-born John than Glooskap. What Gran says — and I think she has the right of it, myself... What Gran says is that John Archer loved this land so much that the land loved him back, and gave itself willingly into his keeping, and the keeping of all Archers thereafter.

Gran's also got it in her head that John took a Pepperidge to wife, thereby insuring the immediate continuation of Archers, and beginning the long alliance of the families. I'm not about to argue the point with her.

31

However it came about, the end result of is that the Archers are tied to the land, bound and intent on insuring its well-being, placing their own safety a distant second to that goal.

That's how it was in the beginning, anyway. Over time, the blood thins and honor with it — humans are like that — and around about 1868, it was looking like the Archers had hit ebb tide.

It wasn't entirely their fault. The Civil War had an appetite for Archer men — not one came back. The wives — widows — they remarried and moved away, taking their little boys, their daughters, and as much of the family silver as they could carry with them. They weren't of the blood anyway, most of 'em. The one's who were left, who were of the blood, they numbered five: Miss Elizabeth and Miss Caroline Archer, maiden ladies of some considerable age; Grampa Richard Archer, who was even older; Daniel Liberty Archer, a babe in arms — and Lydia.

Lydia was twenty-four years old, a spinster with no prospects. She wasn't bad-looking by the standards of the day, more your strapping, sensible Maine girl who in better times would've made some lucky fella a fine wife. The war, though, it had thinned out the available men in town — Archers Beach was a town by then. For every man that came back, there were three women to choose from, and even being an Archer of the Archers, living in the starting-to-rundown house that was held in trust for her baby brother, Lydia never stood a chance.

She cared about that, I'm pretty sure, else what she did that September doesn't really make sense. There's only so much personal sacrifice that a good steward of the land can be expected to make, and while placing your life between danger and the land. On the other hand, she may not have understood what she was getting herself –

But, there. I'm getting ahead of the story.

What happened that September of 1868, is that a monster of a storm came boiling up out of Saco Bay, and stood off of Archers Beach like a siege engine, throwing everything it had at the shore.

Days, it sat there, never moving, never weakening. Under that onslaught, the town began to come apart. Roofs blew off, carriage houses collapsed; half the boats in the harbor were torn loose from their moorings, and the other half were smashed to flinders.

On the fourth day, at noon, though you couldn't have told it from the light, Lydia Archer left the big house by the kitchen door, and walked down to the sea.

Her bonnet was gone before she'd taken two steps; she was soaked to the bone before she'd gone three. The wind grabbed her hair and like to've pulled it out by the roots, and there was so much water in the air it was a wonder she didn't drown.

Wading knee-deep, leaning her weight into the wind, the rain striking her face hard enough to bruise, Lydia kept walking, and eventually — improbably — she made it to the water's edge.

That would have been on the far side of what's now Grand Avenue, with the storm surge chewing at her boots. She hung on to what was left of a hitching post, and she lifted up her face to stare into the storm.

"Stop!" she yelled.

The wind ripped a row of shingles off the wreck of the bandstand and threw them at her. Lydia raised her free hand to shield her face, and when the shingles had fled up the hill, harried by the wind, she yelled at the storm again.

"I'm Lydia Archer and I command you to stop!"

Well, that was so novel that the Sea Ozali who was at the core of the disturbance stepped right out of the storm, stood on the turbulent waters and stared down at her, amazed.

"You," he said, his sea green curls lying smooth and dry against his brocaded shoulders, "dare to command me?"

"In this," Lydia panted, while the storm continued to buffet and abuse her, "I do. I have — precedence."

"Precedence?" Thin green brows lifted in astonishment. "Explain that."

"I am — Guardian of the Land," Lydia gasped, as the waves, driven by the wind, leapt up to snatch at her waist.

"Oh, and indeed?" The Sea Ozali was, perhaps, amused. After all, it wasn't every day that he was commanded by anybody, much less a mere mortal, who clearly expected it to stick. For a handle on how it must've seemed to him, think about your reaction, if the worms in your springtime garden suddenly rose up on their tails and gave you a piece of their minds.

"How far," he asked, then, because it really was only a game to him, and, truthfully, holding the storm together was beginning to get, just a little, tiresome. "How far, Guardian, will you take your stewardship?"

"As far as necessary," Lydia said, fatefully. "Name your price."

Aeronymous, for it was he, laughed, and the storm began to fray. Hastily, he pulled the trailing edges back, and considered the drenched, ugly mortal, with her brilliant *voysin*.

"Come with me as my concubine of your own free will, and forsake your land forever," he said, taunting her. "That is my price."

"And if that is met," gasped Lydia, undoubtedly in an altered state by this time, "you will go and leave this land in peace?"

Aeronymous smiled. "On my name, and on my power, I so swear."

"I'll come," Lydia said, then, "but I have a condition."

"Do you?" he murmured, so entirely diverted that the rain began to lighten, from a deluge to a downpour. "And what might that condition be?"

"That any child of our union be given the freedom to return here at their majority, and, if they are wanted, take up the task of Guardian."

"Done!" Aeronymous cried, and held out a hand. "Come to me."

And Lydia — she put her hand in the hand of the Sea Ozali, and walked across the turbulent waves to stand at his side.

He, true to his word, which Ozali can be, now and then — he calmed the waves, dismissed the wind, and stopped the rain. When all was calm and peaceful, and the sun began to glow behind the few remaining rags of clouds, Lydia looked to him, inclined her head –

And Aeronymous snatched them away from Archers Beach, to his palace in the Land of the Flowers, where Lydia did indeed bear him a child before her *voysin* failed and she was gone.

When the boy Nathan reached his majority, Aeronymous, true to his word, as Ozali can be, now and then, set him down in Archers Beach, to determine if the land required his Guardianship.

It didn't; by 1918 Archers were thick on the ground, and the land was well taken care of. However, it was here that Nathan met Nessa Pepperidge, and the two fell in love.

But that's another story.

About the Author

Sharon Lee has been married to her first husband for more than half her lifetime; she is a friend to cats, a member of the National Carousel Association, and oversees the dubious investment schemes of an improbable number of stuffed animals.

Despite having been born in a year of the dragon, Sharon is an introvert. She lives in Maine because she likes it there. In fact, she likes it so much that she has written three novels set in Maine; mysteries *Barnburner* and *Gunshy*, and the forthcoming fantasy *Carousel Tides*.

With the aforementioned first husband, Steve Miller, Sharon has written twenty-one novels of science fiction and fantasy — many of them set in the Liaden Universe® — and numerous short stories. Under her own byline, she has written five additional novels; mysteries *Barnburner* and *Gunshy*; and the Archers Beach fantasy trilogy: *Carousel Tides, Carousel Sun,* and *Carousel Seas.*

Sharon has occasionally been an advertising copywriter, a reporter, photographer, book reviewer, and secretary. She was for three years Executive Director of the Science Fiction and Fantasy Writers of America, Inc., and was subsequently elected vice president and then president of that organization.